W9-ADL-311

APR 2 2009

A Beginning-to-Read Book

I Did It, Dear Dragon

by Margaret Hillert

Illustrated by David Schimmell

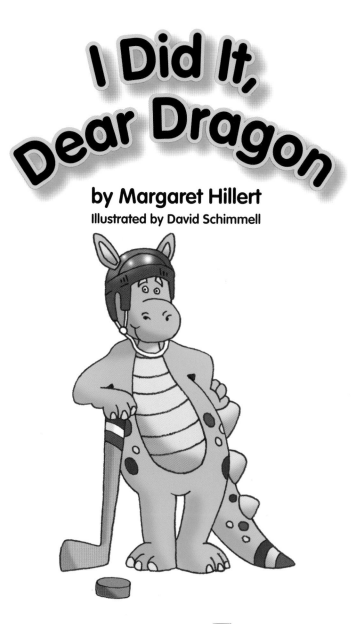

NORWOOD HOUSE 🏠 PRESS

DEAR CAREGIVER, The *Beginning-to-Read* series is a carefully written collection of classic readers you may remember from your own childhood. Each book features text comprised of common sight words to provide your child ample practice reading the words that appear most frequently in written text. The many additional details in the pictures enhance the story and offer the opportunity for you to help your child expand oral language and develop comprehension.

Begin by reading the story to your child, followed by letting him or her read familiar words and soon your child will be able to read the story independently. At each step of the way, be sure to praise your reader's efforts to build his or her confidence as an independent reader. Discuss the pictures and encourage your child to make connections between the story and his or her own life. At the end of the story, you will find reading activities and a word list that will help your child practice and strengthen beginning reading skills.

Above all, the most important part of the reading experience is to have fun and enjoy it!

Shannon Cannon

Shannon Cannon,
Literacy Consultant

Norwood House Press • P.O. Box 316598 • Chicago, Illinois 60631
For more information about Norwood House Press please visit our website at
www.norwoodhousepress.com or call 866-565-2900.

Text copyright ©2009 by Margaret Hillert. Illustrations and cover design copyright
©2009 by Norwood House Press, Inc. All rights reserved. No part of this book may
be reproduced or utilized in any form or by any means without written permission
from the publisher.
Designer: The Design Lab

LIBRARY OF CONGRESS CATALOGING-IN-PUBLICATION DATA
  Hillert, Margaret.
   I did it, dear dragon / by Margaret Hillert ; illustrated by David
Schimmell.
      p. cm. — (A beginning-to-read book)
   Summary: "A boy and his pet dragon play a game of hockey in the
snow"—Provided by publisher.
   ISBN-13: 978-1-59953-295-0 (library edition : alk. paper)
   ISBN-10: 1-59953-295-6 (library edition : alk. paper) [1.
Dragons—Fiction. 2. Hockey—Fiction. 3. Snow—Fiction.] I. Schimmell,
David, ill. II. Title.
   PZ7.H558Iam 2009
   [E]—dc22   2008035941

Manufactured in the United States of America.

Come see this.
See it come down, down, down.
It is so pretty.
And we can play in it, too.

I have to put this on—
And this—and this.

Mother. Mother.
Look at us.
We will go out now.

Do this. Do this.
We can make something.
Something funny.

Look at this.
It looks like you.
Now we can go play a game.
Run, run, run.

This is the spot.
This spot is for a game.
A good game.

And this is a spot for you.
You will see how we play
this game.

I have to have this on.
Now I can play the game.

Here we are.
It is good to see you.
I want to play with you.

Here I am.
Give it to me.
Give it to me.

Here I go.
Away, away, away.

Oh, oh.
This is not good.
Oh, help, help.

Help me get up.

Oh, my. Oh, my.
Look at him go.
He is GOOD!

Look at that.
Oh, no.
This can not come in.

I have it.
I have it.
Now see what I can do.

Here I go.
I am good at this.
I will make it go in.

Here it GOES!

Look at that.
I did it.
It went in!
It went in!

Oh, what a good game.
It is fun to play with you.
It is fun to have friends.

Here you are with me.
And here I am with you.
Oh, what a happy day, dear dragon.

The following activities support the findings of the National Reading Panel that determined the most effective components for reading instruction are: Phonemic Awareness, Phonics, Vocabulary, Fluency, and Text Comprehension.

Phonemic Awareness: The /ē/ sound spelled ey

Oral Blending: Say the /ē/ sound for your child. Say the following word parts and ask your child to say the new word made by adding the /ē/ sound to the end:

hock + /ē/ = hockey   monk + /ē/ = monkey
k + /ē/ = key   chimn + /ē/ = chimney
donk + /ē/ = donkey   vall + /ē/ = valley
mon + /ē/ = money   turk + /ē/ = turkey

Phonics: The letters e and y

1. Demonstrate how to form the letters **e** and **y** for your child.

2. Have your child practice writing **e** and **y** at least three times each.

3. Write down the following and ask your child to add the letters **ey** in the spaces:

mon_ _   k_ _   turk_ _   hock_ _   hon_ _   voll_ _

4. Read each word aloud and ask your child to repeat it.

5. Ask your child to independently read as many words as possible.

Vocabulary: Story-Related Words

1. Write the following words on sticky note paper and point to them as you read them to your child:

puck   helmet   goal   block   skates   ice

2. Mix the words up. Say each word in random order and ask your child to point to the correct word as you say it.

3. Mix the words up and ask your child to read as many as he or she can.

4. Ask your child to place the sticky notes on the correct page for each word that describes something in the story.

5. Say the following sentences aloud and ask your child to point to the word that is described:

- Hockey is a game that is played on _____. (ice)
- The boy put on a _____ to keep his head safe in the hockey game. (helmet)
- In hockey, the goalie's job is to _____ the puck from going into the net. (block)
- Hockey players wear _____ to move across the ice quickly. (skates)
- The players move the _____ with sticks and try to get it into the net. (puck)
- When the puck goes into the net the team scores a _____. (goal)

Fluency: Echo Reading

1. Reread the story to your child at least two more times while your child tracks the print by running a finger under the words as they are read. Ask your child to read the words he or she knows with you.

2. Reread the story, stopping after each sentence or page to allow your child to read (echo) what you have read. Repeat echo reading and let your child take the lead.

Text Comprehension: Discussion Time

1. Ask your child to retell the sequence of events in the story.

2. To check comprehension, ask your child the following questions:
- What did the boy and the dragon do in the snow?
- What are some other things you can do in the snow?
- What things did the kids need to play hockey?
- Describe a time when you were a part of a team. How did you all work together?

WORD LIST

I Did It, Dear Dragon uses the 69 words listed below.
This list can be used to practice reading the words that appear in the text.
You may wish to write the words on index cards and use them to help your
child build automatic word recognition. Regular practice with these words
will enhance your child's fluency in reading connected text.

a	fun	in	play	want
am	funny	is	pretty	we
and		it	put	went
are	game			what
at	get	like	run	will
away	give	look(s)		with
	go		see	
can	goes	make	so	you
come	good	me	something	
		Mother	spot	
day	happy	my		
dear	have		that	
did	he	no	the	
do	help	not	this	
down	here	now	to	
dragon	him		too	
	how	oh		
for		on	up	
friends	I	out	us	

ABOUT THE AUTHOR Margaret Hillert has written over 80 books for children who are just learning to read. Her books have been translated into many different languages and over a million children throughout the world have read her books. She first started writing poetry as a child and has continued to write for children and adults throughout her life. A first grade teacher for 34 years, Margaret is now retired from teaching and lives in Michigan where she likes to write, take walks in the morning, and care for her three cats.

Photograph by Glenna Washburn

ABOUT THE ADVISER Shannon Cannon contributed the activities pages that appear in this book. Shannon serves as a literacy consultant and provides staff development to help improve reading instruction. She is a frequent presenter at educational conferences and workshops. Prior to this she worked as an elementary school teacher and as president of a curriculum publishing company.